Delusions

Brent Matley

Copyright © 2024 Brent Matley

All rights reserved.

This is a work of fiction. Names, characters, places, and incidents are products of the author's imagination or used fictitiously. Any similarity to actual persons, organisations, or events is purely coincidental.

2nd Edition

"I dedicate this novella to my mum, Adele. Throughout life she has been my everything, without her love and support, I would not be the person I am today. To my nan, Valerie. I hope you are looking down upon us with the angels, may we meet again one day."

> *"Is it a crime if the victim is fundamentally evil?"*

Chapter One – A Repetition of Nightmares

It makes me sick, travelling through these streets gazing ahead at the veneer of the neon lights knowing what is on the other side. The smell of dirt, grit and steam coming up from the underbelly perfectly encapsulating life here; survival. We cross over at the security gates, into the seemingly so-called paradise. Detective Alain glances over at me, worried for my alertness.

"You half-awake or what? Rough night?"

I assure my partner of my capacity to do my job.

"You should know by now, I'm always rough, full of pessimism and painkillers, still, it seemingly fuels me to carry on."

Alain lets out a wry smirk.

"I should've known by now I'd get an answer like that, well, like I always say, a healthy lifestyle must envy you. We are not far now, I'll let you read over the brief."

I begrudgingly take the report knowing what awaits me, the denizens of this lovely city putting their best work on display; we are the gallery visitors. Euphoria, 2085; the city which has everything; the ultra-rich are nigh on immortal, with a near 150-year life expectancy, while the poor fight amongst each other for scraps in the slums. Corporations rule the ever expanding and the everlasting black skies of night with holographic searing advertisements, ready for the next consumerist fad, for who can afford it. What is left of the old world is the decaying French architecture juxtaposing our corporate overlords.

I scrutinize the report, two businesspeople, male and female, have been found dead by hotel services in Hotel Merlot. Reports from staff suggest the victims died suddenly, pools of blood were found emanating from their mouths, it seems no struggles were present, and no lacerations were immediately spotted from the staff who discovered them.

"Remind me again of the names of the victims and their backgrounds? Detective Angelo."

"We have Layla Stone, daughter of Brendan Stone, second in command of Stone Industries; a now global operation, they serve many governments in the redevelopment of districts, ushering in 'a new prosperity for humanity.' Next up, we have Cain Roth, Layla had been dating Cain for some time, near upon four years. Rumours had always been swirling she was dating him due to government connections;

Roth was the most senior architect in Euphoria city council."

"I guess power surrounds itself with power, no surprise they were closely linked."

Detective Alain and I arrive on the scene around 2:30am, we both exit our state issued Victorious police vehicle, once more into the fray, the sleek black paint of the Victorious perfectly matching the heart of this city; I felt the coldness while on duty, I felt the grasp of the ether pulling me towards the darkness every time, I have spent years trying to forget, it never lets me go, the events of that night still haunt me, I have been hollow ever since.

Despite all the pain and torment, Alain, and I, have suffered over the years, we always made sure we kept a razor clean appearance; I always wore my trademark marron plaid suit, complimented with my ever-reliable marron mac, gold cufflinks and pristine black dress shoes. Precinct regulation suggested we keep clean shaven and stately, I got away with my 'gentleman' moustache; everyone on the precinct respected me and knew it was my trademark, but I have always been a stickler for the rules.

Detective Alain had a penchant for coloured suits on the other hand; on duty he wore a scarlet-coloured matching three-piece suit complete with a sterling silver pocket watch and ruby red shoes. He was a tall chap with an imposing stature, he had short curly hair and was clean shaven, he wore small round spectacles. Alain has forever had a distinctive appearance.

The precinct mantra was "in order to conduct our duties effectively, we must strive towards pride in our appearance." This phrase was used as the bullshit jargon for us to toe the line, make us look like good police officers. The reality of it was, most of the force took the easy route, loopholes, bribes, pardons, you name it. I was still determined to do my duty, let me tell you; I'm no saint, I've done things that would make the devil welcome me with open arms, I just cling on to hope, hoping there is still a glimmer of good left in there.

Alain and I make our approach into the hotel.

The Merlot was striking; one hundred floors of opulence, themes of ruby were engrained in the décor, from the penthouse suites to the corridors. Beat cops had already arrived on the scene and had started cordoning the hotel lobby.

I approach one of the officers with haste.

"Who's the officer currently in charge here? We are Detectives Angelo and Alain."

"Sgt. Cadell sir, he's just over by the reception desk, the chaos has settled now, he'll be able to give you some more detailed information."

Looking around in the lobby, the remnants of the unbridled panic of guests leaving in a hurry. It's funny in a sense, how shielded some of these people are, blissfully unaware this 'unbridled panic' is a regular everyday occurrence for those poor families in the slums. Once we scoped the lobby enough, I give Alain the nod to take the lead as we move towards the Sergeant.

"Sgt. Cadell, I believe? It's unfortunate we meet in these circumstances, I'm Detective Alain and this is my partner, Senior Detective Angelo. Can you tell me what you know so far?"

The officer obliges.

"Certainly, detectives, reports from two room service staff who were on the 71st floor at the time, where the victims were staying in one of the penthouse suites. Around 12:30am room service was in the vicinity of room 109, both staff heard two sudden loud thuds and the sound of glass shattering. They called and knocked a couple of times but got no response, they radioed their manager and were advised to enter using their key cards to ensure the wellbeing of the guests. Staff found both victims slumped over a glass table with blood gushing from their mouths. Drugs and booze were part of the victims plans this night, but I think we all know this wasn't the cause of death. Mind you, I heard forensics saying their thoughts, saying there isn't much to go on at first glance."

Alain was now engrossed in detective mode, like a sudden lightning bolt, he was now engaged. He begins his stringent line of questioning.

"Do we have the names of the two staff who discovered the body? Where are they now?"

"Their names are Christopher Haliday and Elizabeth Baston; they are currently in the back staff room of reception with the trauma team. Both are a little shaken up, but they should be able to still talk."

"Thanks for the info, Sergeant. I presume then, forensics have already closed the scene and took samples?"

"Yes, they have, once you have both spoken to room service, you can head on up to the suite. Oh, and one more thing detective, that high end private investigator Amaris has been snooping around, you'll probably bump into her at some point."

Alain thanks the Sergeant for his help.

Ah yes, PI Amaris, she has been around for years, paid by the big corporations to do their own 'private' detective work. She is exceptionally good at what she does, never plays any sides, a mercenary of sorts if you will. Amaris has been a pain in the precincts side for years now, using money and connections to get where she needs to be. She operates without jurisdiction, something we could only wish for on the force, to bring justice to where it rightly deserves to go.

We head in behind reception to question the witnesses, both were quite visibly shaken by the experience of discovering two freshly concocted dead bodies. After a short while, you become completely numb to death; every scene, every investigation, becomes like the everyday monotonous task, like doing the laundry or making breakfast. Everyone knows the psychological effects, but what we forget working in this line of work, just how haunting finding something like this is; a lifeless vessel of what once was. The trauma team was still with them, I have always hated this aspect, but it's necessary in what needs to be done. I take the lead this time.

"Christopher Haliday and Elizabeth Baston? I'm Detective Angelo and this is my partner, Detective Alain. I'll cut straight to the chase, I empathise with the events which have transpired tonight, but we need to get to the bottom of this, would you be able to answer a few questions?"

Both parties look visibly dead themselves, the colour has vanished from their skin, only to be replaced by a colour resembling the cold white frost of winter; their eyes hollow now, robbed of innocence. Knowing this and feeling it, I still needed to push on.

They look at each other hesitantly, either not wanting to relive it, or not wanting to be involved, it was too late for that now.

I respond with an affirmative yet empathetic tone.

"To do our jobs properly and to bring the killer to justice, unfortunately, we need to go through the chronological happenings of tonight in detail. Will you help us?"

Christopher and Elizabeth both nod together.

"We will help your investigation as best we can. I think I speak on behalf of Chris we're both scared witless, nothing like this has ever happened before. Now we are both involved, how can we know we will be safe from suffering the same fate?"

"I can assure you both you will be on strict round the clock police watch if you agree to testify, we will have armed police officers on standby and you will be relocated in a safe location."

I gave the usual spiel, even though what I said was true, I knew as well as anyone; if a killer such as this wanted you dead, they would find a way without question. A part of me hates saying it, I can feel my inner being clawing its way to my heart. I should tell them the fucking truth. Despite how I feel about it, my statement gives them the reassurance they needed to hear. I begin my line of questioning.

"Now you've both settled a little, can you walk me through tonight, step by step and going from when you reached floor 71?"

Christopher takes the lead.

"It started off like any other Friday night, we have around twelve teams of two which operate on floor sections, me and Elizabeth have floors 70-79 to serve for the evening. We start the shift at 6pm and we start finishing around 1am. Nothing was out of the ordinary previously the whole evening on our shift, we started winding down for the night and doing our last rounds. We were serving the guests in room 102, a few doors down from 109, as we were heading back to the elevator, we heard two tremendous thuds and the sound of glass smashing. We called through around three or four times and we got no response, this was near 12:30am; we radioed the manager explaining the situation, they radioed us back advising us to enter using our room key cards, this was around 12:45am; that's when we discovered…"

"That will be enough for us, thank you for your co-operation."

Elizabeth exhales a great sigh of relief we don't make them go through what the victims looked like at the scene once again.

I reassure them one last time.

"We will be in touch if we need anything else, please keep in contact with our trauma team in the meantime, you will be able to go home shortly."

"Thank you, detectives."

Now we had dealt with the witnesses, we were free to head up to the room itself. We enter back through to the lobby, Sgt. Cadell escorts us to the elevator where we can head up, he gives me the key card so we can access the room. Forensics had showed up to analyse the scene at 1:30am, with the technology available now, emergency services can investigate in the blink of an eye. The forensics team use highly advanced drones equipped with infrared and UV cameras, to built-in chemical analysis scanners; however, us mere mortal detectives still have an advantage in one area; we can connect the dots and think outside the box.

We make our ascent towards room 109, as the elevator opens the hallway looks pristine, except for the disarray of mess created by the evacuation of the guests of course, nothing looked out of the ordinary. Alain and I approach the front door; no signs of forced entry, we both agree. The suspect or suspects may have gained entry another way. We enter the room.

The plan of action was to examine the victims in detail first then meticulously search the room in detail for anything we can find. The victims were both distortedly slumped over the grand golden coffee table, blood, now dried, painting their faces unashamedly. The diamond encrusted glass broken. Everything else in the room was seemingly untouched at first glance; the silk rouge curtains, the decadent bedrooms filled with silk rouge bedsheets and golden décor, everything coordinated, matching the theme.

Layla was wearing a deep noir dress, complimented with a projection necklace; I examine it with my gloves, it was a picture of her with her father, she was younger here, in her early teens. Her lifeless body now contrasting her dress; a perfect symbiosis of black and white. Cain was wearing a dark emerald coloured suit along with matching waistcoat, I noticed the awfully expensive looking watch on his left wrist; it was karat gold, an engraving of the Stone-Industries logo sat inside the face of the watch. The watch must have been a gift of some sorts due to their previous work together. Both victims irradiated wealth, but now their young, lifeless faces lay painfully on this floor.

We both examine the bodies in detail, no lacerations were present of the face and neck or on the body, as the clothes were intact; no signs of a struggle ensuing or any strangulation marks, no immediate breaches of entry. The only remnants present were the drugs and booze littering the place, I surmised, was this an overdose? Both victims coincidentally collapsing at the same time. It appears it was made to look this way.

"What do you reckon so far then?" Alain wanting to know my thoughts just as much I wanted to know his.

I gave him my thoughts.

"It seems no-one breached or entered the room, no-one was in direct contact with them at the time of death, and, despite all the drugs littered about, I highly suspect they've got nothing to do with it."

"I completely agree, it seems the killer was proud of their work, take a look at this note I found in the pocket of Cain's blazer."

Alain hands the note to me, it was written on fine bamboo; the writing on the card was in French, it was now considered a dying language. Alain's heritage could help me out on this one. The card read:

"L'ordre légitime sera restauré, les opprimés de cette ville auront leur voix entendue. Nous venons pour eux."

"Do you have any idea what this means Alain? Quite unusual for our killer to know French these days."

I hand the card back over, Alain stood constant momentarily, he knew French quite well back in our early days on the beat together, but we haven't heard anyone speak it in years.

"I think it says something like order being restored, the poor being left for so long, I think it potentially alludes to their plans. I have a feeling more people are next on the list."

"So, we could have a network out for their own personal style of justice, they've taken two elite players. We must find out who's next on their list."

Alain looks onward internally conflicted.

"Let them have the bastards I say, a few less of these leeches would do the world a favour!"

I shared his sentiment, we do our jobs but most of the time, it doesn't feel like the job I imagined when I was young and naïve; destined to defend those who needed it most. The corruption runs so deep, the Euphoria City police department feel like an extended arm of paid corporate bodyguards. We spend much of our time babysitting the rich.

Now we have examined the bodies we have a deeper look around the rest of the suite, a large, extravagant glass pane overlooked the city; the glare of the city lights, holograms and traffic almost acting as a reflection. I carefully inspect the window using my UV torch, there were no cracks, scrapes, or any certain breaches. No-one entered this way. We look around at the ventilation shafts in the suite; in the bedrooms, in the kitchen and in the main living area, again, no visible sign of anyone entering on this night. Alain and I were almost certain, no-one had been present alongside the victims in their suite.

"Forensics will have the composition of the blood ready for us tomorrow, and any other relevant information they find. Let's wrap up and pick it up back then, we're walking corpses."

I agreed with Alain, we had spent around three hours examining, leading into the early hours of the morning. I never slept much anyways these days, home for me was purgatory. Still, we all need some reprieve away from the hell of this role, even if it's just a continuation. We head back out and the leave the suite just as we left it, ready for the forensics and coroners to collect the bodies and anything left for analysis. The hotel was now devoid of all civilian life, the officers that were left were finishing up their duties for the night.

We exit back from the elevator and through the lobby, as we exit the main entrance, we spot none other than PI Amaris still prying around, she greets us with her signature sultry yet deceptive tone.

"Good morning, detectives, having fun, are we? Always so late to the party, does the department need more money to do its job? Maybe I could teach you both a thing or two."

"No surprise you're still snooping around, corporate paying you the big bucks again?"

"You know me so well Angelo, I was in the area at the time, so my handlers only seen fit to put my skills to use once more; I have my own investigation to conduct."

"Figures you're still in the game, ever get tired of working for these poisonous pricks?"

Amaris smirks slowly, she recognises who she works for, she doesn't care.

"We all must get by somehow, I'd love to stay and enjoy our little chit-chat but I'm a busy woman, besides; you both look like car wrecks anyway. Pressures of the job getting to you both? It must be, you're both wearing it."

Before we could even retort, she disappears almost instantaneously, like a spirit bound for the afterlife. Amaris was always sleekly dressed, her tied back raven hair matching her tanned complexion, her lipstick matching her matte black suit and skirt; she even walked and swaggered with a concise pace, like time was her master. She was continually on the move.

"She is a fiery one! Keeps us on our toes."

"That's what worries me, Alain."

We enter back into Victorious ready for the journey back home, we exchange pleasantries and call it a night.

Chapter 1.1 – Home

I finally arrive home, apartment 27b. I drudge myself up the seemingly infinite number of staircases to greet my door, the elevator is busted half of the time, so this walk after a long shift only adds to my ever-diminishing physical health. I turn the handle wearily and enter, the pitch-black silence a constant shadow and reminder of what awaits me every time I finish my shift. I had five or six hours to get some rest before heading back into the station, the time now was 7am.

I turn on my dimly lit lights, the yellow tinge gives me a warm feeling momentarily, I flop on my well-worn couch, the grooves of it welcome me back with open arms. I have comfort for a moment. I rest for a good ten minutes before shifting myself to get up and make a sleep-tea. I brew the kettle and prepare the tea, I gaze longingly out of my window desperately wanting the past, wanting it to cocoon me, wanting it to transport me to better times.

I miss them.

Looking out over the Melrose district is a relentless reminder of the scars and suffering we all have had to bear. The civil war of 2075 erupted which eventually led to the revolution in 2079; we were all promised a better life, but that never came. History has taught us all too well of what too much power can do. The asteroid which hit in 2070, changed the atmosphere forever; parts of the Earth became unhabitable; large concentrations of Sulphur Dioxide formed in pockets all over, humanity survived through sheer will and perseverance. Shortly after the asteroid hit, the 'united' governments of the world panicked, this led to immense poverty; food shortages, electricity outages and massive harmful gaseous storms hammered the planet.

Now in 2085, the big corporations allowed the rich to survive and flourish once again. The corps now have more money and power than the governments, rendering them useless. The people of the world who are in severe poverty have been left permanently behind, or so it seems in this bleak future. Crime rates in the slums of the city are astronomically high, murders, thefts, muggings, arson, you name it, they all occur on an hourly basis. The police are significantly overwhelmed, so we leave them to kill each other like rabid dogs. I question it every day, and I question my loyalty to the force. Will times ever get better? It's getting harder and harder to cling on to hope as each day passes, the more torment I see.

The ping of my kettle wakes me up from my vacant thought, I sit down with my tea and try not to think anymore, I eventually drift and slumber, I become an empty vessel for a few hours away from the harshness of reality.

Chapter Two – It Begins Again

I awaken to multiple loud thuds on my door. It was Alain, his voice ringing, vibrating around my room.

"You awake partner? Get your arse up, we're due at the station for two."

I fumble in the dark, my blinds still shutting the world out. I look at my clock, it's 1:30pm; shit, I hurry up and get myself dressed.

"I'll be out in a moment." He knows my character by now.

It was a hack job, but I manage to get myself out of the door in some fashion.

"Smelling fresh as a daisy as always Angelo, I'm surprised you're not wearing your breakfast." Alain was being his usual jovial self.

"Har, har, very funny. Sorry we can't all look immortal like yourself."

Alain chuckles, once we finished chitchatting it was straight to business; the day was monotone grey, a heavy downpour had started around 8am but I was too tired to even notice, this continued up to now.

We traverse down my apartment block steps and get in the Victorious; forensics would have the composition of the blood by now. Travelling through the Melrose district is a relentless reminder of the not-too-distant civil war; bullet holes still lie stubbornly in building structures, the beautiful French architecture of what once was, decaying, crumbling ever slowly, wearing the scars of bombs and hatred. The Melrose district was only slightly better than the Underwood district, we are still left all the same.

We arrive at Precinct 21 on time, just. The precinct seemed like a small outpost compared to the overwhelming large population of 'miscreants' we had to police; it was only three stories high and filled with a hundred officers including sixty beat cops, twenty in forensics, ten on admin, which leaves us ten detectives. We all had our work cut out. We enter and head straight up to forensics, I check-in with Perri who the head of forensics division is; she was precise in her craft, as to be expected, she takes no prisoners, she was a veteran. Even though Perri was always in her whites, she had a distinct appearance; her auburn hair and green eyes have probably stolen the hearts of many. I greet her warmly.

"Good afternoon Perri, how are you on this fine day filled with murder and deception?"

She laughs, nothing ever changes.

"Always a pleasure Detectives, albeit never the most pleasant reasons for the visit.

I presume you have both been assigned to the Layla and Cain case?"

"Of course, no doubt putting us on the case, they love giving us the challenging ones. What can you tell us?"

Perri took no comfort in sharing the details, but we all had to become hardened in this line of work.

"Both victims seemed to have died from radiation poisoning, their blood contained a significant amount of alpha radiation; an element called Polonium. This would have to have been ingested by the victims, leading to their demise hours later. Looking at it, it was probably slipped in their drinks or food which had been prepared for them. We shall know for certain with the coroner's report, but this would match up with no signs of a break-in and no use of excessive force. Whoever did this, planned it carefully, probably over a few months, even years!"

Alain and I thank Perri for the information, with how concise the findings were, we head directly into our office to start working. The first order of business was to pay Brendan Stone a visit; we both concluded he would be angry and full of vengeance, these emotions superseding his pain of losing his daughter, due to the man he was. It is important we get to him immediately to get his thoughts on any vendettas anyone may have against him or his family. Brendan operated out of the Primrose district; this was the richest district in Euphoria.

We have a quick cup of coffee to heighten the senses and we head out once again, Brendan resided in Stone tower, he had built an empire; like anyone else with power, he used illicit tactics and aggression to get his way. It was about a five-mile drive to get to the Primrose district; you knew once you got there the corporations ruled. Primrose was guarded all around its district lines, twenty-foot-high concrete walls complete with watchtowers and biometric scanners. The gates weren't even guarded by city police but by a widely used private military faction called ACE. The corps paid them well.

Once we reach the gates, we state our business, and they give us the thorough check our arses run around. Security was watertight, making it even more impressive in a sense someone or a group had managed to poison someone in the Merlot knowing how strict it is even for us police officers with jurisdiction.

Security gave us the all clear to enter, we waste no time in heading straight to Stone tower as soon as we could, we knew Brendan would be operating from an undisclosed location soon given the gravity of the situation. Primrose was filled to the brim with corporate high rises and lavish penthouse suites, you couldn't mistake Stone tower though, it had the Stone trademark logo brightly resting on top of the hundred floor tower. The logo itself depicted a fist clenching a hammer used in mining, it was ironic, the themes of communism contrasting its thoroughly capitalistic nature.

"Look at this district, you can barely breathe, suffocated by towers everywhere you look." Alain remarks. I agree with him, the very nature of the planet all but nearly gone, the lucid green trees I vaguely remember now a distant memory.

I reply in engagement.

"We're not far off being uploaded as some sentient AI robot, we've already lost so much of ourselves which make us human. "Alain and I always had these deep discussions, we had to blow off steam; what was on our minds. We would go insane otherwise. We arrive at Stone tower, Alain takes the lead on this one, we head on in to be greeted by the reception team.

"Good afternoon, I am Detective Alain, and this is my partner Detective Angelo. We need to have a chat with Mr Brendan Stone, it's imperative we talk to him, is he available?"

The receptionist is jittery, unsurprisingly as news travels fast in Euphoria, nothing is a secret anymore.

"Y-yes why certainly, I shall just ring up, bear with me."

She makes the call.

"Good afternoon, Mr Stone, I have two detectives here wanting to speak with you, can I send them up?

We hear the chatter of Brendan through the phone.

"Yes, I will escort them to your office, goodbye Mr Stone. Would you both like to follow me?"

As we follow the receptionist through to the elevator, we soak in the tone set here, multiple plaques coat the walls detailing the achievements attained by the company, triumphs in their eyes such as largest redevelopment of City Hall, Primrose Library and Hospital to name a few; they sound like great aids to humanity until you learn only the citizens of Primrose can access these facilities. We ascend the elevator and approach Stone's office.

"Mr Stone, I have the two detectives here for you."

"Thank you, Emma. Detectives, how can I help? Please take a seat if you wish."

Like the hallways, Stone's office was filled with accolades. We take a seat, Stone's appearance was sharp, he had slicked back silvery white hair, coupled with an expensive plaid patterned suit along with matching waistcoat and luxurious jewellery. Stone had a scar on his right eye, it looked like it was from a previous attack with a blade of some sort. Alain engages in his questioning.

"Thank you, Mr Stone. I am Detective Alain, and this is my partner, Detective Angelo. I know this is a very traumatic time for you, but we need to get to the bottom of why this all happened and if you believe anyone may be targeting your family."

Stone presented as confident and self-assured despite I suspect some internal suffering, after all, he is a ruthless businessman.

"Of course, detectives, I will offer all the help I can give."

Alain proceeds further with his line of questioning.

"May I ask where you were last night, you were not with your daughter in the evening at the Merlot?"

"No, I wasn't, but I was supposed to be. The evening at the Merlot was to celebrate Stone Industries new partnership with City Council to redevelop the Underwood district and tear down those god-awful slums."

We didn't react, but we knew this man had no remorse, he had no remorse for the families who were just getting by, or anyone for that matter who was struggling. Redevelopments such as those planned just made it worse, City Council seen people in the Underwood district as expendable; they essentially threw the population out on to the streets to fend for themselves. They always approved anything that would bring them more financial gains.

Alain continues.

"Where were you? Why didn't you attend the evening?"

"I was attending to some administrative duties; Emma can attest to my presence being here after midnight."

Alain pries further.

"What kind of administrative duties?"

Stone becomes slightly aggressive in his tone.

"If you must know, I was finalising contracts and going over the paperwork for Benson Construction to be the company who gets the go ahead on the redevelopment."

"I see, one final question for now Mr Stone: Can you think of anyone who would have a vendetta or problem with your family or company?"

"Take your pick, the main groups I would think are EALA, the Asuna Corp and Phoenix Corp. The Euphoria Alliance for Liberty for All, directly oppose my interests, and they stand on the extremities of the political spectrum, so there's that. The Asuna and Phoenix corps are in direct competition for me on expanding and redevelopment projects, and we all know, we don't play by the rules. I think you can work out why I think they might have some involvement."

What Stone says matches up, I believe myself and Alain will be of the same mind; I don't believe Stone had any involvement for what went on at the Merlot.

Alain wraps up.

"Thank you for your co-operation, Mr Stone. Once again, I am sorry for your loss."

"Goodbye for now, detectives."

Once we exit the office, Emma escorts us back down to the lobby, here we question Emma to see if Stone's story matches up.

I take the lead this time.

"May I ask you a few questions Emma, before we leave?"

Emma seems very tense still, but I think this is because of the importance of the situation.

"Yes of course, w-what would you like to know?"

I reassure Emma to be calm and to answer each question truthfully and to the best of her memory.

"Were you working here last night and what time were you working until?

"I got here around 5pm, I worked for quite some time helping Mr Stone out with all the important dealings that have been going on recently, that's until what happened last night. I didn't get away from here until early in the morning, I'd say around 1:30am.

"Thank you for the information. I have just a few more questions. My next question is: Were you working upstairs with Mr Stone in his office? When did Mr Stone leave?"

"Yes, I spent the night working with Mr Stone, we both headed back down to the lobby around 1am, that's when he left to go home. I stayed behind for half an hour doing my checks and locking up with security."

It appears Emma may be telling the truth.

"Thank you for your time, we shall be leaving, goodbye for now."

Alain and I leave to head back towards base to discuss our findings and thoughts, as we are travelling back to the precinct, I ask Alain what he thought.

"What do you reckon then? Is Stone innocent?"

"Well, Emma backs his alibi and even before then, why would he do it? He had a great working relationship with his daughter, plus Stone Industries seems have been doing the best it's ever done before this murder."

I completely agreed with Alain on this one, working as a detective for quite some years you get an instinctual sense for people. Having years of experience can help you see through the veil of lies, you never get it right all the time, but trusting your instinct is certainly better than nothing.

We reach the station and park our Victorious back up; we then head upstairs back to our office so we can get to work on mapping this out.

Alain starts to ponder.

"So, who are our players in the game? I was thinking about the corps and EALA before Stone said anything. The EALA completely opposes what Stone Industries stand for, I mean I don't blame them; then, we have the corps who are in direct competition, their moral compass isn't exactly strong."

"It feels obvious to point towards the corps or the EALA, but is it this easy open and close case? Maybe it is, instinct tells me not, we need to investigate further. The coroner's report should be back tomorrow morning, hopefully it will confirm the suspected radiation poisoning. We will get to work tomorrow and connect the dots."

The time now was near 6pm, Alain and I decided to call it a night for now and pick it up again in the morning.

Chapter 2.1 – Alain

I reach home, 77 Mayfield Avenue; my sanctuary. I turn the key and as always, I am greeted by my wonderful wife, Eva. I am still as in love with her as ever after twenty-five years; her rich green eyes, her radiant smile lights up any room. We haven't had it easy, just like anyone else, and we always have our good days and bad days; but we communicate, we work together and try to solve our issues. We have been through some traumatic events; some where I share common ground with Angelo, this made our partnership as detectives stronger, and it has been the key in us solving some tough cases together, we are brothers.

My wife asks me how my day was.

"Stressful day darling? Silly question really, always is for the both of us."

Eva and I both worked within the criminal justice system; however, she used her words and intelligence to take down criminals, better than I ever could.

"Always are the great hair cleansers our professions, aren't they? I'm sure you have seen on the news the high-profile murder at the Merlot. How was your day, my love?

Eva chuckles at my comment, we have enough stress between us to power a small dam, I always pondered to myself, why both of us chose these paths; maybe that's why we were attracted to each other in the first place.

"It was terrible what happened at the Merlot, I presume you and Angelo have been assigned to the case? My day went quite smooth for a change this evening, we have a new paralegal on the team, they started today so I have been easing them in gently so to speak."

I knew Eva's playful nature so I knew she would have toyed with them being the newbie.

"Please tell me you went gentle on the newbie. Yes, me and Angelo have been assigned to the case, think it's going to be a tough one for the both of us."

Eva smiles cheekily as she responds.

"Of course, I did, I'm not that bad, am I? I think she will make a great member of the team, her name is Amy, she has just graduated from Euphoria university with first class honours, so she is sharp. Please tell me you will take it easy on this case, you need to look after yourself still, I know how obsessed you can become."

I reassure her and let her know I will take it easier this time, unfortunately I knew this wouldn't be true, I just never want to worry her. Cases like this one always wrapped their tendrils around me.

For now, we forget the world around us and try to enjoy our evening away from the stresses of our daily lives. We sat down in the evening and enjoyed our dinner together; we made our favourite meal; katsu curry, the wonderful aroma always reminded us of a time when the world was a bit more peaceful, we travelled through Asia together in our youth, we have fond memories of it and having this meal as a treat fills us with the right amount of nostalgia.

We take our time eating, enjoying the moment together, we both communicate and talk so much in our occupations, so we sit in silence for a few minutes; to soak in the silence, our racing minds coming to a halt for a brief instance. After, we longingly lie in bed and just cuddle, we enjoy reading an enjoyable book together before the inevitable rise again into the next workday. I wouldn't change this little slice of heaven for the world.

Chapter Three – Dancing with the Renegades

Thud, thud, thud. My eyes open. Alain knocks on my door once again, here we begin once more, like an old record stuttering.

"You awake yet Mr. Boss Man? I'm getting cold out here."

Alain was always here bright and early ready with his assortment of quips, truthfully, I always enjoyed them.

"I'll be ready in a moment, it isn't like me to make you wait, is it?"

I get dressed quickly and sort my appearance out so I'm not a festering walking rubbish disposal, Alain was always here too early, he can wait. I arrange myself so I'm clean and ready for the day ahead, I'll do for now. I greet Alain at the door, we start heading down to the Victorious. The weather was calm, which was surprising, as we always expected rocky weather due to the state of the world.

Once we enter the Victorious, we look towards our agenda.

"What's the plan for today, Angelo?"

"The report from the coroner will be with us at the precinct now, so we will know for certain if radiation poisoning was the cause of death. We then map out the main players, what do you say about giving Aaron Alexander a visit first? He's the leader of the EALA."

Alain has always taken an interest in the political state of things, hell, we lived through a revolution.

"Aaron always seemed a little extreme whenever he's been featured on the news, it will be interesting to see him in the flesh." Alain was intrigued by his character, we have all seen a lot of him in the media, it will be interesting if he really wants to implement what he says.

We reach the precinct around 9am, we were there sharp, ready to tackle what lay ahead of us; our resilience seemingly running through all the backup stores, we go again and again. We head upstairs to be greeted by Perri, she informs us the coroner's report has been left on my desk; we waste no time in looking through the report; it confirms what Perri, and her team had concluded, the victims died by radiation poisoning.

Alain and I get started on mapping this whole thing out, who the main suspects could be and their motivations for doing so; whoever did the killing had to have powerful connections to pull something like this off.

We start by clearing our board so we can start mapping.

"Well, first on the list is Aaron Alexander, his motivations are out there in the open; he is against these corporate reptiles and what they stand for, judging by what his group have done over the years, this isn't out of their league."

I agreed with Alain, technically on the front of things, himself and his group were the perfect match.

"The other two suspects I'm thinking of are Amaya Himura of Asuna corp. and Troy Davis of Phoenix corp. Amaya is head of security for Asuna, they are pretty much trained assassins under their public guise. Asuna has their hand in everything regarding economic developments, they aren't afraid to use brutal force and cunning tactics to get their way. Troy Davis is the Vice President and practically the brains;

every decision and strategy goes through him."

"A Japanese and American company both vying for the pie, makes sense Angelo them wanting a piece."

Alain and I spent a few hours mapping out possibilities and motivations, the time now was near 1pm; this gave us plenty of time to visit the Underwood district in which Aaron operates out of. The Underwood district had the highest crime rate and the worst poverty, it was no surprise people rebelled once they knew they had been left; the phantom voices crying for their lives to have justice and equity.

We head out in the Victorious around 1:30pm, it doesn't take us much time at all to reach the security gates; it's only a seven-mile drive from the precinct in the Melrose district, but the change is stark, even though Melrose is slightly better in terms of economic security. The security personnel have no problems letting us in to the district unlike in Primrose, however; you would have a much harder time leaving Underwood, especially if you're a 'normal' citizen.

Once we got into the Underwood district and started travelling through its streets, the impact of the state of living here was on full display; many homeless people were out on the streets huddling closely as units to keep warm, buildings were decaying, many left with broken rooftops and shattered windows; only offering little shelter when winter hits.

The hustle and bustle of street dealings, disagreements and violence could be always heard and felt throughout the district, and despite all of this, you felt a camaraderie and community spirit not felt in any other district in the city; the people here have lived through struggles and harsh realities, but they still push through. I admire that.

Aaron operated in the central part of the district, the EALA set their base of operations in one of the attached buildings of a community centre offering food and shelter to those who needed them most. The EALA were formed to fight back, to fight for the forgotten, which won many of the hearts of the people of this district, however; they have done morally wrong and nasty deeds in their recent past, power could corrupt them ever further if they gain a significant foothold, or they could overthrow these corporate thugs and pave the way for a better future. Who knows what to make of this shitshow anymore.

We arrive at their base, I couldn't help thinking back at the card left at the murder scene with the message written in French, this perfectly matches up with their retribution on the privileged elite, we couldn't cast conclusions yet and as detectives we have our own bias, it's our job to shake them. We head into the building, most of their members are moving and shifting supplies to aid the community centre.

The people hated us cops and didn't want to help us at the best of times, but we needed to push on. I ask one of their members if Aaron was here.

"Excuse me, do you mind helping me and my partner, is Aaron Alexander here today? We need to ask him a few questions, I am Detective Angelo, and this is Detective Alain."

The member was a young man, in his early twenties, he looked the picture of rebellion, with the EALA bandana sat proudly on his head, his t-shirt had an emblazoned phrase printed on it saying, 'fuck those who left us to die.'

"What do you want, you wastes? Come to look like you're doing your jobs, you're fucking useless. You only come here when there is a problem for yourselves, not for us."

He was spot on the money really, I had no argument in this situation, on many counts I knew we could do more. I just wish there were more of us to help to make a change. Despite this, we needed to get our man.

"I don't disagree with you, and I know many of you hate us, but we need to speak with Aaron regarding a recent murder I know you would have all seen by now. If you believe your leader is innocent, you need to let us through."

The member pauses for a moment, he looks sheepish in his decision, his mind torn.

"Alright then, we've got nothing to hide anyway, he is upstairs in the operations room. You'll find your way easy enough."

We head on through into the building and up the stairs, you couldn't miss Alexander, he was running things with tight precision and leadership, after all, his experienced in the special forces served him well. Aaron had a gritty look and a hard exterior, he looked like he took pride in his battle scars; he had a deep cut scar leading from the back of his ear to his lower neck, he was clean shaven all over. Aaron accompanied his appearance with the tactical uniform of the EALA, they look like a poor version of mercenaries, but you could tell Aaron was a seasoned vet.

We enter the hectic base of operations and introduce ourselves; I take the lead.

"Aaron Alexander, I am Detective Angelo, and this is my partner, Detective

Alain, do you mind if we ask you a few questions in private?"

Aaron hated the sight of us, it was written all over his face, in his eyes, cops were on the wrong side of the history he wants to make.

"Well, if it isn't the cops, wonder why the visit this time? You only come here when the big corpo thugs don't like what we're doing. I'll answer your questions, like every person in the EALA knows, we have nothing to hide!"

Aaron gestures and moves us into one of the smaller meeting rooms.

I start my line of questioning.

"I will get straight to it; we are here to question you in relation to the murder of Layla Stone and Cain Roth."

Aaron retorts.

"Yeah, I heard they were both dead. I saw the news report, such a shame, isn't it?"

His sympathy completely non-existent.

"Can you tell me where you were on the night of their deaths between the hours of 5pm to 12.45am?"

"I was at a rally with the EALA here in our district at the Council offices, funnily enough we were protesting the proposed redevelopment these corpo pricks were planning. We were all there up until around midnight."

I reply with a small but truthful quip.

"Use any assault rifles this time at your rally?"

This riles Aaron a little.

"Well, if words and politeness were of any use in this world you let me know detective, these corpo thugs only know one language. They use it just fine."

I continue my questioning.

"Where were you after midnight? After you left the rally?"

Aaron asserts himself; his tone gets deeper.

"I came back here to the community centre; I was managing our food supplies to hand out to folks the next morning."

"Was there anyone else at the centre at this time, anyone who can vouch for you?"

He looks at me and looks intently into my eyes.

"I was the only one there at this time, if you think I had anything to do with those killings, I didn't. As much as I wished to get to them first, someone else beat us to it, your guess is as good as mine."

Aaron wasn't the type of person to bullshit, but they have used all manner of tactics in the past, especially with his special forces training; he served extensively with the GIGN in his past. This made him deadly; we couldn't be certain of any involvement yet.

I conclude the interview.

"Thank you for your time Mr. Alexander, we may be in contact again."

Aaron smirks.

"Don't worry Detectives, I won't be going anywhere."

We wrap up, we had nothing solid to prove Aaron or any of the EALA had any involvement, except for their organisational values. We start heading back to the Victorious, leaving it for too long in this district and it wouldn't still have four wheels and intact windows, as we head back to the precinct our discussion turns toward Aaron.

"What do you reckon then? I think they could be involved in some way, but how can we prove it?"

I start theorising, every different avenue racing through my mind. I respond.

"I get the feeling this murder was a little too sophisticated for the EALA, they normally use brute force, but with Aaron's training they could have changed their tactics. To breach the building like that, you would need some serious connections on the inside, we can't be sure for certain yet."

We get back to the precinct, we theorise for a little while more and then call it a day for now. We both plan for the next morning, up next for a visit, Asuna.

Chapter 3.1 – Silence

I reach my apartment door once again; the silence hits me like it always does; unexpectedly. The job keeps my mind busy; focused and engaged. At home it's a different story, I feel lost, for hours I gaze without purpose at my desk, at my computer screen, at my walls. Hours passing me by until all my free time is used up. I can't help it, I probably need therapy, I still feel the grief.

I lost my wife and daughter during the 'revolution' in 2075. My darling Nadia, my precious daughter, Lena, both lost in one night. There had been escalating riots all around the city, before this, it was still known as Paris, but by 2065, English was the primary language here and in most of Europe. An organisation much like the EALA, promised freedom and liberty for

Paris, they were known as The New Revolutionaries for Peace and Prosperity. History has proven, many groups such as this do not use peaceful means.

The riots became more violent, more feral. Myself, my wife, and my daughter were at home at the time, it was the night of September 25th, 2075, we heard on the news the outbreaks of violence were getting closer to our home. We were too late. When the rioters stormed our streets, gunfire broke out between the rioters and police as they tried to quell the rebellion.

Our home was invaded and as we tried to make our desperate escape in our vehicle, stray gunfire hit all of us, the frenzied panic afterwards felt like a blur, a fever dream. The emergency services arrived but it was a lost effort, my two most precious humans gone in a blink, they suffered severe blood loss and didn't pull through. Why did I have to survive? Why didn't I react sooner to the news? I thought we was safe, out of harm's way, I never thought it would come to our door.

I failed them.

Once I had come around, I found myself lying in a hospital bed, voices, and memories flashing, pulsating through my mind. The doctor eventually gave me the news when I had the capacity to understand, once he told me, I screamed in anger for hours, the pain suffocating me, the tears drowning my eyes. How do you get over pain like this?

The weeks passed by, the NRPP won and eventually reigned supreme over the government, much like as of today, the French Government used totalitarian tactics to control its people. The NRPP promised the people a new age of liberty, this didn't last long as power corrupted them, and they became what they set out to destroy. Government power eventually weakened, and this is when the powerful corporations seized their opportunity to rebuild and become more powerful than the political leaders.

This is where we stand today, the hollowness of loss and grief slowly eating me each day, the job helps me to try and some good in the world. I focus on putting these killers away, to make a small difference, but I am clouded with confusion and uneasiness, the force is corrupt itself. I feel like I am in a time loop of a forever losing battle. Once again, the hours distort and pass me by. Thud, thud, thud.

Chapter Four – The Asuna Assassination

I awake in the middle of the night, my phone blitzing, two missed calls; it was Alain. He informed me that the chief had been trying to call me, there has been another murder. Only a few days later and we find ourselves amid another killing, Alain informs me an Asuna exec has been found by an Asuna security guard in their business offices with deep lacerations all over their body; they had been stripped naked and tied before the final deathly slit being one found right around the neck. I inform Alain I shall pick him up this time, I get showered and dressed swiftly, as fast as I could with my eyes half-open.

I reach Alain's place and knock on, ready with my own quip this time.

"It's me this time who gets the drop on you. How do you manage to have such perfect glowing skin at this time?"

We still find the time to be jovial.

"With all due respect boss, piss off, I won't be giving out my skincare routine free of charge."

After we banter around, we get to business. The time now was around 3am. I ask Alain to give me the details, what we knew so far.

"A security guard by the name of Charlie Brooks was working the late shift at Asuna business offices in Primrose, some of the business execs work until late so they have security detail working around the clock. Charlie was doing his rounds on the higher floors of the building where he found the office of Jiro Hayashi locked around 2am, with all the blinds down; he knocked on and waited around five minutes before entering, this is where he found Hayashi in this state, tied to a chair with tape around his mouth and the multiple lacerations all around his body. Police were called at 2:05am."

I ask Alain about Hayashi's role in the company.

"He had close ties with Amaya Himura, he was the financial team leader for Asuna developments in Euphoria, he oversaw all the expansion developments they had planned. There seems to be a pattern emerging."

I agreed with Alain, whoever the killer or killers were, two key players in expansion developments were taken down, with more probably on the list. We had to get to the bottom of the why and who fast. The EALA had their reasons, their motive was to get rid of all the people high up, the people who engaged in reforming the Underwood district. In terms of Asuna, why would they target their own? Was it an internal conflict between the high powers fighting for more power? Phoenix could also be muscling in for their piece of the pie. We needed to find out more, no doubt Amaris would be around sniffing around soon; she worked for all the corps, they all pay her to act in their best interests.

We start making our way into the Primrose district once again, always a delight dealing with security. Once we get past security, we arrive at the Asuna business offices at 3:30am, the bright neon red lights sat atop glaring, searing into our eyes. Officers were on the scene, they cordoned off the offices and escorted all personnel out of the premises, apart from key witnesses. We approach one of the officers by the entrance.

"Officer, who is acting in charge here? We are Detectives Alain and Angelo."

"It's officer Robertson sir, he is currently with the key witness who discovered the body. He is just in the room behind reception, head that way, you'll find it."

Alain thanks the officer for his help, we then head in behind reception. Alain takes the lead.

"Officer Robertson, I am Detective Alain, and this is my partner, Detective Angelo. Is the witness willing to talk? Have the trauma team given him the go ahead?"

The officer responds.

"Yes, the trauma team spoke with Charlie, they assessed him and advised him to check in with his medical doctor if he was feeling the psychological effects of what he saw. He was advised support was available if he needed it. Charlie does have a military background, so he probably has a strong mind. He is sat in the meeting room, through this door, head on through."

We head through into the meeting room and introduce ourselves; Alain does the talking once again.

"Charlie Brooks, I am Detective Alain, and this is Senior Detective Angelo. If you wish to proceed, do you mind if we ask you a few questions in relation to the events what have transpired tonight?"

Charlie was tall with a strong frame; you could tell he had gone through military training.

"Not a problem officers, I'll be honest and say I was taken aback a bit when I discovered the grotesque sight of poor Mr Hayashi; I've seen my fair share in my previous tours of duty. I'll be fine, don't worry about me. I know the trauma team can support me if I need it. What can I do to help?"

Alain starts his line of questioning.

"Can you walk me through when you started your shift and when he was due to finish, did you notice anything unusual or out of routine?"

Charlie's body language was confident, he maintains eye contact with us both while answering.

"Well, I got on shift around 8pm, we oversee the offices while some of the Asuna execs stay behind and work late. Employees here check in using ID, even when it is late there are still quite a few people coming and going; to access the building you need executive clearance. Nothing was out of the ordinary so far, but I did notice Mr Hayashi's blinds in his office were shut, this was around 1am. I didn't really think anything of it as many of the higher employees work in private."

Alain explores further.

"When did you suspect something was wrong?"

"I circled back around on my patrol, at this point Mr Hayashi had been working a long time, this is when I knocked on the door to check to see if he was okay. I got no response after multiple calls, this is when I discovered the body, the time was 2am. I called you guys immediately afterwards."

"Did you hear any strange noises, screams for help?"

Alain asks a great question.

"I didn't hear anything suspect the whole time, whoever did this had years of experience, some kind of professional assassin I bet."

It was a fairly accurate guess; Alain didn't give too much away.

"Could be something along those lines. Thank you for your time, you have been very professional considering what has transpired tonight."

We wrap up the interview with Charlie, relieving him from this ordeal for now; we go through the usual steps as always and advise him to stay in contact with the trauma team. Our next move was to head up to the office and examine the scene. What Charlie said interested me, he heard no noise coming from Mr Hayashi's office while essentially, he was being tortured. I made an informed theory; I believe the killer used a paralysing agent to numb the victim but made it so that they would still be aware of what was happening; that had to be the reason I was almost certain of it.

We head up the stairs and enter the office, forensics had already been, they collected blood and fluid samples from the scene amongst their other usual high-tech wizardry of UV light examination. Before we examine the body, we check the outside door and windows for any breakages or struggles that had occurred when the killer entered the room; Alain and I concluded there weren't any signs of forced entry, the killer had access. We then examine Mr Hayashi in further detail, he had been tied to his office chair effectively, and seemingly efficiently; to not even alert any security and to vanish without making any substantial mistakes.

Jiro had been tied to his chair with industrial rope, thick black tape was sellotaped over his mouth; multiple lacerations were all over his body, leading to two deeper cuts around his neck, these were the final blows. His expensive suit and waistcoat tarred with blood. I had a gut feeling Jiro was fully aware when the killer began torturing him, my theory of a paralysis agent being used could be confirmed with the blood samples once they came back.

Our eyes then turned towards examining the room itself; documents of contracts littered the table; I see nothing of note on further inspection but what caught my eye was an open laptop. We were either extremely lucky, or it had been set up this way, the laptop had a password remembrance system so we could access it; I opened it carefully using my gloves as to not tamper with the scene.

Once I was into his network, a page was already open on his emails, something caught my eye; threatening emails had been sent from the enforcement division of Phoenix corp. over the past month or so.

The messages which were sent involved backing off from developments and expansion into territory Phoenix seen as their own; they were warned multiple times to 'stand down' or face further consequences, could this act tonight be a part of their promise? Why would the killer be sloppy and leave this lying around?

It was now the early hours of the morning once again, Alain and I decided to wrap up call it a night for now. We make our final sweeps and head back down to the lobby, who else but none other than PI Amaris to greet us, who was snooping around; she was pretty much casing us at this point, or so it seemed. Amaris was dressed in all black once again.

She greets us with her usual sarcastic wit.

"Good morning boys, still lagging behind it seems, blood has been spilt on your watch again. Not doing your jobs properly, maybe they should hire someone a little more competent."

I ponder my own questions to her while she tries to insult our competency.

"You're always never far behind a crime scene Amaris, how do you get the lowdown so quick?"

She gives her response, always using that sultry tone.

"The big boys pay me to do my own investigations, I have my means and connections. I'm just efficient all-round; I move alone, I'm fast. It will take years for you boys to acquire my skill."

"Charming."

She always did like to talk a big game, she could back it up.

"Well, I must dash, I am investigating Mr Hayashi's death. I am being paid handsomely for it; I can't lounge around like you two."

Amaris moves swiftly upstairs to the offices before we can even respond; the thing is, even though she wasn't police, she had enough power and money to muscle her way to any crime scene. The corruption was rife.

"Lucky to be in that position, have enough backing to essentially go where you want. Makes the force look like fools."

Alain was right.

"I don't disagree, our hands are bonded. We live in a shitty world with shitty rules with shitty leaders. Let's pack it up for now and pick it up again in the morning, I'll meet you at the precinct for 1pm."

"Aye boss."

Chapter 4.1 – Himura

The alarm ringing again, the day begins once more. I meet Alain at our office, we get straight to it. Forensics should have the blood analysis available for us. Before I head upstairs to meet Perri, Alain and I surmise about what we think transpired last night and why, linking it back to the bigger picture overall and the connections to the last murder.

We start by mapping everything out on our board; the EALA were in the picture because of the calling card left at the murder of Layla and Cain; Asuna could still be involved through an internal power struggle; I was thinking this was unlikely, but we needed to find out more from Himura. A day out was on the agenda regarding that particular visit. Phoenix corp. was looking likely in having some involvement with the murders with the evidence of the laptop being left, but this could have been planted by the killer; we didn't know yet for certain.

After we map out and plan and set out our intention of interviewing Himura today, I head upstairs to pay Perri a visit; after we exchange pleasantries, I ask her what the team has found from the results of the blood.

"It seems the victim had been initially poisoned with an extract of highly toxic venom from a poison dart frog, the victim was given just enough of a dosage to paralyse them but leave them aware of what was going on; at least for a short while before succumbing to their deep lacerations. The poison was administered quickly into their arm. It seems the killer entered Mr Hayashi's office and acted swiftly to subdue him this way, my educated prediction is the killer then moved Mr Hayashi and tied him to his chair; this is when they got to work."

I thank Perri and her team for doing solid work, we had a lot to think about. Whoever the killer was, they were a professional. Did the EALA really have an individual or team with this kind of skillset? I still couldn't underestimate them though. Phoenix and Asuna did possess this kind of power. Once we receive the coroner's report again, we will be able to learn more.

We start the day by making our way back out into the Primrose district to pay Himura a visit at the head offices, we enter the Victorious and prepare to make the arduous journey once again. Getting through security was always the most painful part; corporate dummies who lost their soul long ago, whatever orders they are given, they follow blindly.

Once we got through the security we headed towards Asuna tower, most of the corporations were all clustered together in the district. The wealth of display was astounding to witness every time I passed through here; on the one hand we have made so much progress due to technology and ambition, the argument can be made that capitalism can allow an individual to succeed, in which I can see the benefits there. I ask myself this question though; where along the line did we lose our compassion for each other? To at least help one another to have the basic needs to survive? In Euphoria, this world seemed to be long gone.

We arrive at Asuna tower; it felt a little bit more distinct than Stone tower; a substantial projected display of cherry trees was displayed on the main base of the tower; a token to remind the people of their Japanese heritage. Their trademark logo sat aloft much like that of Stone tower though. Alain and I proceed on through into the lobby; it was quite striking, a small manmade waterfall sat in the middle of the lobby, displays of Japanese history were encased all around the lobby, it was fascinating. Once we stopped admiring for a brief moment, we went into our detective modes; we were seasoned pros now at talking with the receptionists.

We talk with the receptionist and question whether we could see Himura, they were expecting us anyway. The receptionist escorts us into the elevator, which took us up to Himura's floor, she knocks on her office door respectfully and awaits Himura's response; she slowly opens the door and greets us with a smile; but don't be fooled, Asuna had built an empire, and you don't get that by playing nice all the time.

Himura was in her early fifties, she was elegant and was dressed in a floral business suit, it had the Asuna family crest woven into the suit, she wore this alongside a gold and ruby dragonfly brooch, another signature of Asuna. She had a warm face, but I could imagine this would soon change if you ever got on the wrong side of her. Alain takes the lead on this one.

"Good afternoon detectives, what can I do for you today? I presume you are here to talk about poor Jiro. Such a shame what had happened to him and what a distasteful way of doing it."

"Good afternoon, Mrs Himura, I am Detective Alain, and this is my partner, Detective Angelo. Unfortunately, we are indeed here to talk about the murder of Mr Hayashi at your offices. Can we start with what your relationship was like with Jiro?"

Himura's body language appeared quite open, she seemed happy to discuss and engage with the first question Alain asked. The question was tame however, let's see how she reacts when we initiate the heavier questions.

"Of course, Jiro was my most trusted right-hand man in a sense. He handled our financial expansions such as district redevelopment and all the statistics and data analysis of profits and where best to distribute our money; but I am not blind, I know not everyone may not have their best intentions for you as you do for them; that is why Jiro worked still part of a closely knit financial team."

Alain presses on.

"Can you just expand on what you mean by best intentions? Was there friction in-house at Asuna?"

Himura becomes a little tighter lipped, but she still seemingly reveals her truth for now.

"I trusted him, but my late father did not. My father, Akira Himura, was one of the cofounders of Asuna corp. alongside Kenji Asuna himself. My father alongside Kenji built their way up, their hard work; they prided themselves on this company. Once my father sadly passed away Asuna was entrusted to me, my father warned me about Jiro when he was on his deathbed; he whispered to me that Jiro would bring the downfall of the company and to always keep a close eye on him. I always have ever since."

"Did you still trust him up until his death?"

Himura becomes irritated with this question.

"I watched him for years and he never put a foot wrong, unless he superseded all my intelligence and double crossed me and Asuna, but I don't think so. Mind you, in recent times we have taken a bit of a hit financially, but I don't blame Jiro for that."

Alain butters her up after that question.

"Apologies as I have to pry, do you mind if we move on to another set of questions?"

Himura still looks pissed off.

"Certainly."

"Did you have any other threats or recent events from anyone outside Asuna who could have targeted your team?"

"Take your pick; The EALA are constantly hounding us and disturbing our operations for obvious reasons; they have firebombed our warehouses and stolen some of our supply trucks, but nothing on the level of this, but maybe they are stepping it up a notch. Phoenix and Stone are our biggest competitors, alas, it seems Stone have been targeted also. We have had history with Phoenix but it's more on the level of espionage; I believe they have their own spies amongst our ranks. Phoenix do play dirty, and I could imagine them pulling something off like this, they are crazy enough to go this far."

We had enough information to learn from for now, Alain concludes the interview.

"Thank you for your time, Mrs Himura, we will be in contact if we need to speak with you again."

Himura's body language relaxes again.

"Thank you, detectives, my aide will escort you out."

We head back down and out through the lobby and enter our Victorious, as we're heading back to the precinct, the discussion turns towards the interview.

Alain pitches his thoughts.

"What do you reckon to all that then? I reckon there could be something more regarding the friction between herself and Jiro, something she isn't fully letting on."

I respond with my thoughts.

"I believe there is something beneath the surface also, her father didn't trust him for a reason, maybe he was a deep planted mole all along from Phoenix. Maybe his intention was to slowly start ruining Asuna from the inside out. I think we'll know more tomorrow when we pay Troy Davis of Phoenix a visit."

"I wouldn't put it past Phoenix, they've been up to all sorts of sneaky shit for years. Sounds a plan boss."

We reach the precinct after we talk through our thoughts, we settle for a little while and both have a cup of coffee, unwinding from our lives as detectives; a reprieve from the day which lay ahead of us tomorrow.

Chapter Five – Troy

Another day breaks, I meet with Alain at the precinct, and we head up to our office, the coroner's report was awaiting me on my desk. The report confirmed Perri's theory, Mr Hayashi was injected first with a paralysis agent; a dangerous extract from a poison dart frog; then the following lacerations were the ultimate cause of death. Honestly, I did not think Jiro was tortured to gain any information, I think he was tortured in a sadistic fun kind of way. I'm hopeful we will find out the reasoning soon.

We got to work immediately, our agenda for the day was to visit Troy Davis. Troy operated out of his home estate in the small remaining suburbs on the outskirts of the Primrose district, they had twenty-four-hour security patrolling with assault rifles, they didn't take lightly to visitors. It was early in the morning, so a visit in the morning may take them a little bit by surprise.

We got in our Victorious and head off once more into the Primrose district. Once we got past gate security, it was on to another layer at the estate. The ultimate magnates lived in the suburbs, while been surrounded by relative greenery, it was a stark contrast to the claustrophobic neon streets of the city; your senses being bombarded at every turn; here, it was more peaceful, something which the average citizen couldn't comprehend anymore.

We drove up to the estate, two large golden-plated gates protected the driveway up to the main building of what was a mansion; subtlety wasn't their strong point, they proudly flaunted their wealth on full display.

I press the buzzer at the gate. A gruff voice responds abruptly.

"State your business."

"We are police officers, I am Detective Angelo, I am with my partner, Detective Alain. we would like to speak with your boss, Troy Davis. We believe Troy resides here."

The voice responds in the same tone, again with a short answer.

"Oh yeah, and why would you like to speak to my 'boss.' I heard he is a busy man."

I respond shortly also; we didn't have the time to mess around.

"We need to speak with your 'boss' about a recent murder of a high-end exec, I'm sure you've heard about it on the news, so I suggest you stop fucking around and let us in."

My tactic works and he lets us through, but he gives us one last message.

"You can come in, but you ask your questions and leave, no snooping around elsewhere or we will shoot you on sight; we aren't afraid of the police, you are on private property."

We drive on through and go up the winding path up to the main building. The estate was surrounded by multiple exotic trees such as the dragon tree and exotic conifers; these trees weren't just for show, but to tactically obscure the view of the estate, I had to commend them, it was quite clever really. We got closer to the main building and security got tighter and tighter, multiple armed guards now surrounded us.

We parked up just outside, two of the guards were there to greet us, it wasn't much of a greeting; they escorted us through the main building, as myself and Alain walked through, it was extravagant; shimmering chandeliers dotted the ceilings, the décor emitted richness; the theme was pure white mixed with expensive golden decorations and statues.

We walk in through to the main meeting room escorted closely by the security; Troy was expecting us. Troy was quite the stature of a man, he was six foot five and had a muscular build, but do not be deceived; he was a highly intelligent man and as cunning as ever. His appearance was impeccable.

I introduce myself and Alain.

"Good morning, Mr Davis, I am Detective Angelo, this is my partner, Detective Alain. Do you mind if we ask you a few questions?"

He responds in a sarcastic tone.

"Not at all detectives, and I suppose if I did mind you would both be inclined to carry on anyway. Do be careful though gentleman, you have entered my domain now. You are on my property."

Alain chirps in.

"Making threats, are we? I didn't figure you were the type."

I back my partner up further.

"With respect, we are here to do a job. You are powerful, but please remember, our station knows our location and where we are, so two dead policemen wouldn't look so reputable on your public image now would it?"

Troy ponders for a moment.

"Go on then, get on with it. Ask me your questions."

I put on a good poker face; I wasn't going to let Troy see I was intimated. I could see Alain standing firm too.

I proceed to conduct the interview.

"Tell me about the operations you are involved regarding Phoenix? What is Phoenix currently involved in, specifically; financial expansion."

Troy looks expressionless, he wasn't giving anything away.

"Like any other big corporation vying for their own slice, we were involved in district redevelopment just like Asuna and Stone; in my opinion, we do it better. We see the bigger picture, so that is why we have developments in pharmaceuticals, food, and drink; not forgetting we provide the very equipment and vehicles Euphoria police use."

The corruption runs deep, he had a lot of people in the pockets of Phoenix.

He continues. You could tell he loved the sound of his own voice, textbook narcissist.

"Asuna and Stone will eventually fall, it's only a matter of time, what we have over the both of them is multiple expansions into new ground, all of them succeeding."

"Very well, the rumour circulating is that you have many 'moles' within these corporations getting an inside look, could you share your thoughts on that?"

Troy's expression changes a little, he is on the defensive now.

"Absolute nonsense, we haven't planted anyone. What the team and I have done, is cherry picked each best mind from each corporation to best serve us. We offered them about the deal, and if it is a crime to steal prospective skilled workers away, then you can arrest me on the spot."

I press further, dialling up the pressure as much as I could push it without getting us in harm's way.

"But you have used aggressive tactics in the past, haven't you? You're quite good at scaring people. Changed up your tactics this time?"

Troy snarls at us in response now.

"It has all been speculation, nothing of our history has been proven, we are clean cut. You can't prove a thing. May I please remind you of what I promised earlier."

I ignore the threat and call the bluff; it was too risky for them to do anything now.

"So, you don't know anything about the murder of Mr Hayashi? Threatening emails were sent from Phoenix asking them to stand down regarding a redevelopment."

"I don't know anything about the murder, only the information I have seen from the news. It's a terrible shame what has happened, and as for the threatening emails, yes it was true it was about a redevelopment, but we do everything above board; it was a threat for them to stand down or we would be forced to take legal action."

I conclude the interview.

"Thank you for your time, Mr Davis, we will be contact again if we need to do so.

He responds assertively.

"I can't say it has been a pleasure detectives, however, Phoenix has nothing to hide. I will be here if you need to contact me again. My security will escort you out."

I didn't buy anything Troy said, but would they take the risks of being caught in a murder such as this? They had so much power though, they had everyone in their pocket almost. Phoenix used their weaponry and brute force in the past, but nothing ever stuck, we were fighting the biggest uphill battle.

We are escorted by his glorified henchman back to our Victorious, they watch us with their guns pointed as we enter our vehicle; these corps were not afraid of anything or anyone; their power ruling and corrupting had gone to their heads. We start our journey back towards the precinct.

Alain shares his thoughts with me.

"They are crafty bastards them lot aren't they; always up to no good behind closed doors covering their tracks. Whether they are involved in a brutal murder such as this, is another matter."

I respond with my own thoughts.

"They aren't giving anything away, I mean look at the hardware they are flaunting, they are cocky because they can get away with it in their own backyard. Even with their ego, they are smart and deceptive when they need to be. Nothing yet proves their direct involvement, we need to be smart about it and investigate further. We need to tell few about our next move, not even the chief."

"Definitely, they think with their show of force they can intimidate us, the corruption in our own force is rife. We will fight through it though, for what cause, I don't know; I kinda like someone taking out these corps, even if it is one of their own."

I didn't disagree with Alain, you had to think the people who have been left behind were gaining traction; to fight back against the system, even if it wasn't in the best circumstances for the powers that be; maybe it was necessary for real change to occur.

We arrive back at the precinct, we got to work for a few hours, we put in a solid effort of mapping our next move. We finish up for now, we have a break before leaving for home, our conversation turns towards our personal lives.

"How is Eva doing these days?" I asked.

"She's doing well, thanks for asking boss. You know what the daily stresses are like though, we both work stressful jobs so when we get home; we strike a good balance and try to forget our days, if we didn't, I'm sure we be at each other's throats. How about yourself away from work boss? I'll be honest with you, sometimes I worry about you."

He was right, my life hasn't taken the best turn, but I was slowly finding the determination to improve my own personal life. I couldn't keep wallowing in self-pity, I can't change the past.

I thank Alain for his concern in my response, I reassure him I am making a change for the better.

"Thank you, Alain, for being the most dependable person upon whom I have ever relied. I've been a mess these past few years, but I am going to make a change. After this is all over, I'm going to book myself into some therapy."

"That's great to hear Angelo, you know I'm always here if you need to vent, or just a friendly ear."

I appreciated Alain a lot, when you've been through dangerous times, it made us brothers. We wrap up and call it a night. I had two days off now, so I could get some much-needed rest.

Chapter 5.1 – Tensions Rise

I awoke in the middle of the night see the glaring flashing lights of a news reports on my TV; riots have broken out in the city again, history repeating itself in front of my very eyes; bad memories. Now I was awake I heard a lot of commotion outside of my apartment; people hollering and screaming, glass being smashed and cars screeching.

The news report said a man had been needlessly killed outside of the security gates in the Underwood district, a small group been protesting about the living conditions and about the lack of help from the government. A security guard shot one of the main protestors when they stepped a little closer to the gates, he got shot two times; one in the lung, and one in the stomach. The victim eventually died in hospital in the early hours of this morning.

This had been the catalyst, the final tipping point.

My phone starts ringing, it was the chief, there had been an anonymous tip another murder had occurred during all the commotion, another high-profile victim. I got up and got dressed straight away, I told the chief I give him a call back shortly to get more of the details. Right now, I needed to meet up with Alain, I give him a call and inform him of what has happened, we agree to meet up at the precinct; we needed to be careful though, the city was a hot zone right now. So much for my days off.

Chapter Six – Three Times Lucky

I call the chief back before I left, I had to admire the timing for the killer or killers to strike again when everyone had eyes elsewhere. The anonymous caller disclosed the location of an abandoned warehouse in the Underwood district, where the victim was currently residing.

Was this the killer or group toying with us and playing games? Did they want to be caught? We had to be extremely careful in the way we approached this. I told the chief we would handle it and investigate it ourselves, there was no time; the chief told us the risks of doing so, but I felt a duty to see this through. It had to be us, not some other corrupt schmuck, even if inside I was dreading what awaited us, worst case scenario ending up dead.

I call Alain back and make him explicitly aware of the situation and what we were potentially heading into, I said to him, he could walk away and not get involved in something like this; he said he was with me until the end, whatever happens it's a risk we take. We were both of the same mind; he would do the same for me as I would for him, if something happened and one of us with us wasn't there to try and prevent it, we could never forgive ourselves, we were partners until the end.

Alain and I were prepped to meet at the precinct, we were bringing weaponry and armour for this one.

I get in my Victorious and race to the precinct. The city was burning. Driving through the streets, rage and determination were the two emotions on display tonight; the downtrodden were fighting back, I admired this in a way, but I couldn't help thinking, how many innocent people will be caught in the crossfire? Taking me back to that night, the pain spreading through my heart like a plague. History repeating itself. I drive past towering infernos and emergency services trying but failing miserably to contain the situation, putting their lives on the line.

I could feel the adrenaline, I try to make it to the precinct in one piece, I had to! I could never let cases slip by me, thinking about it deeply, I hope this one does not lead to my downfall. I drive through the city getting many stones and rocks, even molotov cocktails thrown at my car; fortunately, they miss, and fortunately I do not get shot upon.

I finally arrive, somehow. I park my Victorious as safely as possible around the back of the police station in the secure car park, it was relatively untouched for now, I knew it wouldn't be for much longer if we didn't hurry. I grab my revolver and start making my way up to the office, I seen Alain's Victorious parked up, I was praying he made it here unscathed.

The station was eerily quiet, every beat cop had been reassigned to emergency deployment, it was just a skeleton crew now; this left the station pretty much unprotected though. I open our office door; Alain was there waiting for me.

"You make it here okay Angelo? It's a nightmare out there. We're lucky we even made it, driving in our police vehicles with a giant target on our head."

I try and give our morale a boost before we headed back out, we needed it now more than ever.

"We are made of tough stuff, of course we made it. Plus, we have a job to do, we need to close this case for good."

"Of course, boss, let's get to it."

We head down to the armoury with swiftness and grab bulletproof vests for ourselves, we take two flashlights and helmets with a face shield. We were prepped as we ever could be, we go back down to the police parking and take my car.

The address for the warehouse was Unit 3 on Hurst Road; it was part of the industrial estate and was one of the most dangerous places in Euphoria in normal times. It was still the dead of night, so we head out quickly to make our way there, hopefully there was still time to save any potential victim; but realistically, there wasn't much chance.

We were now geared up and ready to take on what awaited us, I didn't like our percentages; we run down into the police parking and get in our Victorious. We open the gates ready to head back into the

Underwood district, or what was left of it. Driving through the streets looking at the havoc and terror of robberies, arson, and shootings, it felt like a lost cause getting the city back under control. Alain and I finally reach the security gates, it was completely abandoned, left unmanned; aside from the haunting images of some the security guards hanging motionlessly above the gates; their souls shackled and sent to wherever they may be.

We approach the gate especially cautiously, driving very slowly through; fortunately, it looked like whichever group came through here had now moved on, probably into the Melrose district. We were through, we didn't want to waste anytime hanging around anywhere for too long, I don't think we both fancied being sitting ducks. Burnt out cars littered the roads, creating blockades, we would have to manoeuvre around. I could feel the beads of sweat dripping down my face. I drive through carefully but with a sense of urgency all the same, the adrenaline surging just waiting for an ambush. Luckily, the industrial estate it wasn't too far from the security gates.

I drive through multiple wreckages along the way, the sound of gunfire and chaos dotting the district frequently. We finally make it, Alain, and I breath the greatest sigh of relief we have both ever done. I pull up our car as much as out of view as possible. The grungy and dilapidated warehouse was covered in darkness, except from the towering blazes littering the corporate district in the backdrop vista.

We exit the Victorious and turn our flashlights on and take out our weapons; it was quiet for now, but who knows who could turn up at any moment. Alain and I both walk gently up to the entrance of the warehouse, we scout around for multiple entry points; two large rusted double doors falling off the hinges block the way, but they were our best bet; due to the way they were standing, there was a small opening where we could get through. We both had to be careful getting through however, as I had a feeling the doors could collapse on us if we created too much movement getting through them.

We discuss how we were going to get through them.

"I will go through first and test whether we can fit though with our dimensions, I'm sure we probably can, I've lost about a stone this night alone I don't know about you Alain."

I still had time for wisecracks and so did Alain.

"I don't know Angelo; we've got some thermal insulation on us still in our old age."

Once we got done with the wisecracks for the moment, I make my approach to the doors slowly, crouching my body as much as I could, climbing through the grime and dirty water which has accumulated; it was an exceptionally tight squeeze, but I managed to make it through. It was Alain's turn next.

I give Alain a hand through, holding the door as much as could so the potential of it giving way would be less; fortunately for us, we both make it through unscathed, albeit a little muddy. I'll take that scenario rather than coming to any harm yet. We start exploring, the moss coated walls a reminder that no-one has touched this place in years, what little we could make out of the dust coated machinery was that this warehouse functioned as a robotics and AI manufacturer many years ago.

The main floor was littered with heavy machinery from a bygone time, so we edge through slowly, we go upstairs to the office rooms; we explore many of the rooms, but we didn't find anything of note, there was one last room at the end of the main corridor. We shone our lights towards the door, it was ajar.

I gently peer through the door, there was a glimmer of light shining through a broken skylight. We walk in slowly, we shine our flashlights toward the central part of the derelict office room, there was a man tied to a chair with a gag in his mouth; we couldn't tell if he was alive or dead, so we edge closer, my heartrate at an all-time high; my firearm ready. His head hung lowly, I gradually raise his head to check for a pulse, but it was too late; a bullet hole was rooted in the middle of the forehead. I shine my flashlight on the victim to identify them; it was none other than Brendan Stone, everything had come full circle; each person on our list taken one-by-one, the only people left standing were Himura and Davis.

We go through thoroughly in our search as best we could in the darkness, other than the obvious lethal bullet wound to the head; he had deep lacerations almost to the bone, on his legs and arms; a few of his teeth were also missing. Brendan's suit was bloodied, there was a small basic metal table which had been placed next to him with a pair of pristine expensively branded black gloves; a note lay on top of the gloves.

I approach the table carefully, my hands sweating profusely as I pick up the note. I open it to a confession of sorts; this is when it hit me, the black gloves reminded me of Amaris, she always wore this brand. A light bulb pops, she was always so close by at nearly every crime scene, hiding in plain sight, I wondered how she always got there so fast; it was right in front of us this whole time. I start to ask myself why she has done this? Has she gone rogue?

I start to read the confession hoping to make sense of it all. An expression was written at the top in French.

> *"Est-ce un crime si la victime est foncièrement mauvaise"*

"What does this mean?" I ask Alain in the hopes that he will know.

"Looking at it, I think it means something like 'is it a crime if the victim is fundamentally evil?' Read on, see what else it says."

I continue to read on; the rest was written in English.

"I'm sure you've figured it out by now Angelo, it was me all along in plain sight,

Amaris. I have been there watching your every move, watching you both trying to work out which corp was fucking over which. I have set out what I have wanted to achieve, but there is still so much work to do. The world is broken, I'm tired of working for these sadistic, twisted, and power-hungry fucks. I have committed terrible acts on innocent people on their behalf, but no more. I must correct our future history. The word has spread, and the new revolution is dawning again.

Who will miss these money hungry sociopaths? All they care about is self-preservation and coming out on top, no-one really loves them, and they love no-one either. The families, the homeless, the downtrodden; they have the compassion, they have the humanity and empathy to care for one another. They deserve a chance. The world needs to change, and this is the only way to do so.

I know you're both going to try and stop me, but I know deep down you know I'm right; I know you feel the same way; are you not tired working for the system? Supposedly working for justice, yet injustice rules every day. I ask of you to let me finish my work, all the history we have lived through together, Angelo. Let me do this, otherwise I may have to act against you. I do not want to go down this path opposing you, but I must achieve change no matter the cost.

Yours always,

Amaris"

I stand there for a moment, taken aback after what I have just read. I hand the note over to Alain so he can have a read. I say no words; my mind and my heart are deeply conflicted, the way she has killed these people viciously and deceptively; I could see the point Amaris was making, there needed to be a change and she believes violence is the only way of doing so. The events she has created have been a catalyst to get another revolution started like she said, she has set out what she wanted to achieve while sacrificing herself for the cause. Amaris was only going to go after two people next; we just had to figure out which one; Himura or Davis. My money was on Himura, I was praying my guess was the correct one.

"I can't believe we've been looking in the wrong places all this time. We can't save both so we will have to guess we go after the right one."

I agreed with Alain, we had to act quickly to try and catch Amaris.

Chapter Seven – Revelations

We were done here, there was no time and no resources to clean up and evaluate the crime scene fully. We knew enough now, and we were on our own tonight. Alain and I exit the office room, we still had to be careful exiting the building and using the stairs, they were about ready to collapse.

We walk down gently, passing all the rusted heavy machinery and making our way towards the entrance, we couldn't afford to get trapped in here. I use the flashlight to the best of my ability until finally, I see the glimmer of the opening where we first entered; we approach slowly making sure to climb under as athletic-like as possible, but we weren't young men anymore.

I manage to squeeze through, but as Alain is climbing through, the doors begin to buckle; I grab hold quickly, putting all my weight on stop the door momentarily. Luckily, I hold it for just enough time for Alain to get through, I let go of the door; the minute I let go it slams down furiously, into the ground.

"Bloody hellfire, that was a close one. Thanks for grabbing the door."

Alain was very grateful.

"That's what partners are for, eh?" I reply.

"Too right, it's a good job we make such a great team!"

This scenario perfectly illustrated why you should always up someone watching your back. After I help Alain back to his feet, we dust ourselves off quickly and we start running back to where we parked the Victorious; another lucky stroke, it was still sat there unscathed. Alain and I get in promptly, I start the engine and start heading towards the Primrose district while trying to avoid the chaos the city was enduring.

We formulate a plan immediately.

"Who do you think she will try and hit next, Angelo?"

I respond with my gut reaction. I was wishing my hunch would be the correct one so we could put Amaris away, however; I was conflicted between my duty between the force and possibly for the greater good of humanity. Things did need to change; these greedy bastards were a good start if I was being honest with myself.

"I have a gut feeling she will go for Himura first, Asuna and Stone we're both vying closely for the redevelopment of the Underwood district, I think it would have been close to her heart; the terrible plans they had for evicting all those families out into the cold with nowhere to live."

"If that's what you think, boss. I will trust your instincts."

Himura will be hiding out in her estate in the Primrose district, I drive on, trying my best to avoid the hotspots of gunfire and sounds of large groups. We couldn't get bogged down, otherwise we were unlikely to survive the night; not that our odds were the best taking on Himura and Amaris.

I head through the city and reach the suburbs; nearly every house was raided, the people who used to live there, long gone. Windows and doors were completely obliterated, every valuable item looted; the citizens of Primrose have had their peaceful and save lives eviscerated tonight. It was deep into the early hours of the morning now, the fires raging on, lighting the night sky.

I drive a little further in, until we reach Himura's compound. There were still many looters in the vicinity, I pull up the car in the least conspicuous spot I could find across the road facing the compound. We had to do a little reconnaissance first. I root in the back of my car to find a cheap pair of binoculars to use, they were makeshift, but they would have to do. I pull them up to my face to have a look at the compound, I look beyond the gates to see what looked like the remnants of a security team still holding out; they had automatic weaponry, but it looked as if they have been thinned out by trying to combat all the rioters tonight, only around eight to ten remained.

A few of the soldiers lay injured on the ground. I pass the binoculars to Alain, to have a scan for entry points and to also see what he can see, and to see if I have missed anything.

"I think our best chance is to sneak around the back and try to find an entry point there. We can't tackle it head on, there are still too many guards who will see us. Only thing is, we can't get a good sight line on the back properly, there could be a small detachment still watching the rear; if so, we will have to take them out quietly. Amaris could be inside already; you know how sneaky and agile she is."

Alain was right, our best bet was to try and move around the back, quickly but silently. We exit our vehicle and crouch down beside it; we walk gently across the street trying our utmost to avoid the sightlines of the security guards.

Alain and I both make it to the outer wall of the compound, we start moving towards the back; I climb up gradually onto a disposal bin and peer over, making sure to expose only the smallest amount of my body. I see two guards patrolling the garden and the path leading to the conservatory into the main part of the house. The guards split into two different directions, we make a quick plan to jump over when the time was right to subdue the guards; they were both now at the furthest point from each other, we act in haste, and I sneak behind my guard and knock him out using a chokehold as does Alain. We pick up the guards and hide their bodies in the bushes to make sure we will not be discovered yet.

It was clear now to proceed ahead, we walk up to the conservatory double doors; they were fully transparent, fortunately for us, there was no-one guarding directly inside. The doors were locked, but luckily for us our police training taught us valuable lockpicking skills; I pick the lock and we both enter inside.

Alain and I decide our best plan was to sweep upstairs and then move downwards to the ground floor, avoiding any unnecessary conflict along the way. The main building of the compound was large enough, guards could be watching any spots and chokepoints including the stairwells. The electricity was off now due to all the anarchy, this was a benefit but also a hindrance to us as we didn't have any access to night vision; we were just as blind as the guards, luckily their forces had been worn down significantly.

We make our way slowly down the hallway leading to the stairs; Himura's mansion was filled with many Japanese artefacts and relics, the ones we could make out in the darkness were expensive. A few of these relics could be sold and the profits could feed an entire family for the year. I understand deeply why Amaris went down this path. We stop at the end of the hallway just before the stairs leading up to the bedroom; there was a singular guard holding his position at the bottom of the stairs.

I acted quickly before the guard turned around towards us and noticed myself and Alain, I snuck up behind him and subdued him, there was no time to hide the body. Now, the pressure was mounting severely, we walk up the stairwell with our pistols raised looking upwards for any guards patrolling; it was strange, there were no signs of any guards on this floor. Alain and I both reach the second floor; it became clear to us now; Amaris was here. Dead guards were tucked in closets as we progressively explore the bedrooms, Amaris must be using a suppressed weapon.

The master bedroom was at the end of the hallway; its door looked like it had been shut tight; again, we raise our weapons in anticipation. I approach the door gently; Alain was directly behind me, my heart rate pulsating wondering what was on the other side. I turn the handle softly and peer through. A silenced pistol was gazing directly into my eyes, Amaris was holding Himura, she had a gag in her mouth, but she was still alive.

"I was wondering when you both would finally catch up, I knew you couldn't leave well enough alone. Always sticking to your duty for what? To police this dying world?"

Amaris was right, we were content to idly stand by accepting the world for what it is. For us in the force, we were complicit in our own way by letting the corruption stand; we could have stood up more to make a change, to do what's right.

"Do come in and close the door behind you, we need to talk."

Amaris wasn't going to give up now, she had come too far, I knew she wouldn't rot in a prison. This was the endgame now.

I respond, full of guilt and sympathy for the situation Amaris finds herself in now.

"I understand why, I know you're not going to give up. I know you are prepared to die tonight."

"Correct as always Angelo, I hope you understand why I had to do it. No-one else had the courage to make a change, the recent revolution seemed a distant memory for most. For a brief time, we had paradise; the people were liberated; there were fair opportunities, fair pay and an individual's rights were treated with the greatest respect. Don't we deserve another shot at it? Yes, power corrupted as history has taught us, but I don't believe we are always destined to live the same lives stuck in a loop. We must try, I believed this was the best way of doing so, if I have to sacrifice myself, then so be it. I'm tired of living in this world and working for these despicable human beings, that's why they deserved a taste of their own medicine."

I am full of conflict and sorrow, I have known Amaris a long time, I didn't want it to end like this.

"You still tortured and killed these people, but I understand; you wanted an eye for an eye, you wanted to give them a taste of what they have done to many innocent people."

A singular tear draws slowly down her cheek, we both didn't want to be in the situation, but fate has made it so.

"Just put the gun down, Amaris. We can work something out."

"You know as well as I, the time has passed. I will be killed anyway; I may as well go down fighting. Goodbye Angelo, I hope you and Alain are now prepared to make the changes in the world, I hope your eyes are open now."

Amaris draws her pistol towards Himura's temple, she squeezes the trigger, dispelling a bullet; she then turns the pistol towards herself, I scream but it is already too late. The two bodies slump to the floor as I hear the rushing of the security guards. My eyes heavy, I am taken out of the world temporarily, so much loss I have witnessed. I didn't want to end this way.

The guards burst into the room; Alain and I both yell and holler signalling we were police officers just after they breach, we hold our badges up as they point their automatic weaponry at our faces. I honestly believed this could be it.

The dust and smoke kicks up into the air, disorientating us; fortunately, they didn't shoot on sight. We explain to the guards what events have transpired in this very room. There was a strange calmness to it all now, who would have believed it led us to this? The mixture of emotions bubbling inside of me; hollowness then anger, at myself; I should have connected the dots sooner, but I don't know what I would have done differently; It seemed Amaris was destined on this path no matter what, and while what she done was cruel and unthinkable, she may have just started the change we truly needed.

We wrap up with the guards and start cordoning the room ready for backup; it was a chaotic night, but this was an urgent matter, I was hoping they would arrive soon.

Alain and I have a breather for a moment while we wait, we try to collect our thoughts.

"What a crazy night eh? I don't think I'll forget this one in a hurry. We are living through history, will be something to tell the kids in the future."

Alain was right, it was another night to add to our growing collection of near misses, it's probably not good for the heart.

I express my heartfelt emotions with Alain.

"I just hate the way the cards had folded; I wish we could have tried to persuade Amaris sooner. She didn't have to die tonight, but I don't think anything would have changed her mind. I'm just tired of seeing loss."

"Don't beat yourself up about it, there's no rhyme or reason to these things sometimes. All we can do is try our best and try to do what's right. It was her decision, and her decision alone to do what she did."

I express my thanks to Alain for bringing me back around, we walk outside the compound to see backup had arrived. We spoke with the officers and were relieved for the night, authority seemed to be grasping back control of the city steadily; Alain and I say our goodnights and we start to head home. I needed to sleep for a good long time, another chapter closed, and another case etched into my memories.

One thing I knew for certain; this case took a piece of me forever.

Chapter Eight – An Uncertain Future

I wake up the next morning in my bed at home, the events of the night felt like a drunken blur in a sense; I didn't even remember coming home after we were relieved of duty; I was on autopilot driving back; I felt devoid of life. The time now was around 3pm, so I groggily get up out of bed to make myself a coffee to wake myself up, I fall onto my sofa like I have been tranquilized myself; my legs too weak to carry my body; I was physically and mentally exhausted after the events of last night.

I turn on the television to see a news report on many of the events which had occurred during the mayhem; Himura was mentioned alongside myself and Alain; we were labelled as the two 'hero' cops who solved the case; we certainly were not by any means, in fact, the loss and sorrow I have endured has made me feel the worst I have ever felt.

I was determined to stay positive, Amaris taught me one thing though; I, like many others, have been an idle bystander and we can all change the world for the better. The news report continued; many of the high corporate execs were specifically targeted last night also, Troy Davis was taken from his estate and all his security team exterminated in the process; I had a feeling the EALA would have had a hand in that, he was found hanging in the middle of the suburbs, on public display with the noose tied firmly around his neck.

The authorities and private security forces had finally got control of the city, but it felt different this time.

Whatever Amaris had started, we were now in an uncertain future, but I had hope; the hope that now people were not afraid to stand up to the big corporations and the corrupt governments of the world.

Euphoria had witnessed the revolution, it had endured many hard times, but when were we going to see the good times? Didn't we deserve this now? Many people have suffered and are still suffering. I knew whatever lay ahead of myself and my partner; we had to tackle corruption in the force and hold these big corps accountable for their breaches of human rights; we need not be afraid anymore, to stand together as a whole, as human beings being compassionate for one another.

Amaris took her stand, we now needed to take ours. She would be known as a cold-blooded killer, but did she really set us all free? The shackles were off.

I get a call; it won't be long until I am back in the fray. This time, I was a changed man.

Acknowledgements

I would like to thank my mum, Adele, for loving me and guiding me, my entire life. I cherish her every day of my life; she is the reason I am the man I am today. To my sister, Zara, I love you very much, please be your wonderful self always. To my beloved nan, Valerie, I hope you are watching over us, I miss you every day; I miss your smile and your laughter deeply. I wish you were still here to witness life; I wish I had the chance to show you, my work. I hope you are enjoying yourself in Heaven, you were my angel in life.